Battle Scars of the Redeemed

Stories of Wounds, Faith, & Being Made Whole

Book 1 of The Living Church Chronicles

Melissa Dyess

ISBN: 979-8-9937579-0-2

This is a work of fiction. Any resemblance to actual persons, living or dead, or actual events is purely coincidental.

Dedication

To God—
 the Author of every healing, every breakthrough, every page.
 Thank You for taking what was broken and making it beautiful.
 This book belongs to You first.

To Becky—
thank you for taking these pages and shaping them into something beautiful, but even more for the love and friendship you've given me along the way.
Your presence in my life is one of the truest blessings God has ever entrusted to me.

To my mom—
 thank you for giving me love, and for planting in me a passion to seek our Heavenly Father more deeply every single day.
 Your faith became the foundation of mine.

To my husband—
thank you for all your love, and for being exactly who God needed you to be to shape me more fully into His calling.
Your strength, patience, and steady heart have helped mold mine.

To my family—
thank you for your encouragement and constant support as God wrote this work through me.
Your love gave me space to listen, heal, and obey.

And to every person along my journey who allowed God to use their story to shape mine, your courage, your scars, and your honesty became my lessons. Thank you for letting your life whisper His truth.

May He receive every bit of the glory.

Table of Contents

Foreword:

A Church Without Name Tags

This is not a book about characters. This is a book about people; people you've worshiped beside, prayed for, wept with… or maybe became or you are becoming.

You'll find names scattered throughout these pages, Elias, Hadassah, Selah, Jalen, but they are not the point. Their names serve only as mile markers in a deeper journey. One that traces the silent drift of a church losing its song, and the sacred return of a people who remember who they're singing to and for.

The ones who leave. The ones who stay but stop kneeling. The ones who pray from a distance. The ones who rise quietly, with trembling hands and restored worship. You may recognize them. You may be them.

Each chapter is a window into one sanctuary, but many hearts. It's not about tracing storylines, it's about waking up. Waking up to the ways we trade surrender for performance. Waking up to the presence of God that never stopped calling. Waking up to the sound of repentance, unity, and real revival.

So as you read, don't just look for characters. Look for patterns. Look for postures. Look for the part of the church that lives inside of you. Let every window, every altar, every whispered prayer… become a mirror.

~Missing Piece Virtual Solutions,
  on behalf of the author

Prologue

The Under Shepherd's Awakening

Elias: The Pastor Who Forgot How to Sing

2 Chronicles 7:14
"If my people, who are called by my name, will humble themselves and pray and seek my face and turn from their wicked ways, then I will hear from heaven..."

Pastor Elias had grown tired.

Not of God, never of God. But of the silence that clung to the sanctuary, even when sound echoed off its walls. The choir had thinned. The piano bench sat vacant more Sundays than not. Praise once lifted like a flood now trickled in like hesitant rain. The people still came, but not in spirit. They attended. They observed. But they no longer worshiped. Elias had prayed. He had fasted. He had even tried to lead the songs himself, his voice cracked with more ache than pitch. But the air still felt heavy. Oppressed. Like the heavens were brass.

One Sunday morning, long before the people arrived, Elias knelt at the altar. Alone. Burdened.

"Lord... am I failing them?... Am I failing You?"

His hands trembled. His voice broke.

"I can preach, but I can't break the yoke."

That's when he heard it.
A soft trill. High and delicate.

He looked up. In the stained-glass window, a bird.
Small. Unassuming.

Radiant in the morning light where the golden cross cast its beam.

He had seen it before, always when worship began.

 But today, it came early.

Today, it came for him.

In that sacred stillness, Elias wept.
Not out of defeat. But repentance.
Not for some scandal or secret.
But for carrying the weight of worship alone.

He had prayed for a breakthrough, but never invited the people to seek with him.

He had sung to fill the silence when he should've taught them to listen.

So Elias rose.
Not with drama. Not with thunder.
Just... changed.

The next Sunday, there were no announcements. No clever welcome.

He opened with a whisper:
"Today, we repent. As a church. As a people.

I have tried to praise God for you.
But worship belongs to all of us.

The altar is open, for anyone ready to return."

What followed was not loud. But it was holy.

The pianist came forward, tears streaking her cheeks.

The oldest deacon lifted a hymn that hadn't been heard in decades.

Teenagers stood, stunned by the power in the room.

And worship returned, not just as sound.

But as a surrender.

The bird returned that Sunday, too.
Not at the beginning.

It waited until the voices blended in unity.
Until the Spirit moved like wind across water.

And then it came.
 Perched in the light.
At peace. 
Just as it always had.

Endurance

2 Chronicles 7:14
"If my people, who are called by my name, will humble themselves and pray and seek my face and turn from their wicked ways, then I will hear from heaven…"

Reflection Reading:

Elias's exhaustion came from trying to stir what only the Spirit can bring. He prayed, fasted, and pushed harder — but the breakthrough never came until he surrendered. His repentance was not for hidden sin, but for carrying a weight that was never his to bear.

Revival, worship, and freedom never begin with our performance; they begin with our obedience. The Holy Spirit does the work, but He invites us to humble ourselves, repent, and open the way for His presence. Worship is not meant to flow from one leader to the people, but from the Spirit through the people as one body.

The bird at the window was a reminder: the Spirit moves when the church yields, not when one person tries to manufacture. When we obey and make room, He breathes life into dry bones and brings songs back to silent places.

Prayer Focus:

Holy Spirit, I confess that I cannot stir revival or carry worship on my own. Forgive me for the times I have tried to do in my strength what only You can do through Your power. Teach me to walk in obedience, to yield my plans, and to make space for Your presence. Move through me, through us, and let our worship rise not from effort, but from surrender. Amen.

Journaling Prompts:

In what areas of my life have I been trying to force or manufacture outcomes instead of waiting on the Holy Spirit?

____

____

What would repentance from self-reliance look like in my walk with God today? _______________________________

____

How is the Lord inviting me to step into obedience rather than striving? _______________________________________

____

Who has God placed around me that I can invite into prayer, worship, or seeking His presence together? ___________

____

How can I remind myself daily that revival and breakthrough always flow from the Spirit, not from my own effort? ________

____

This week, resist the urge to "carry it all" or "fix it yourself." Instead, invite others to join you in seeking God's presence. Host or join a simple moment of prayer or worship outside of Sunday service — at your dinner table, during a lunch break, or even in a quiet corner with a friend. Instead of trying to create the outcome, focus on making space for the Holy Spirit together.

As Elias learned, revival doesn't begin with effort, but with obedience and unity. By stepping beyond the sanctuary walls and humbly gathering others to pray and wait on Him, you open the way for His Spirit to move.

Part One

The Bird in the Window

Hadassah: The Watcher of Glory

Luke 19:40 (KJV)
"And he answered and said unto them, I tell you that, if these should hold their peace, the stones would immediately cry out."

Every Sunday morning, just as the first note of praise rose through the rafters, it came.

A small bird, simple gray, nearly invisible against the stained glass, landed in the narrow arch of the sanctuary window. It came only during worship. Never before. Never after.

Not for the sermon.
Not for the offering.
Only for the moment when hearts turned heavenward.
Some noticed. Most didn't.

But Sister Hadassah always did.

She noticed everything,
The chipped tile by the baptismal font.
The silent weeping during "I Surrender All."

The way Pastor Elias lingered at the altar one second longer when no one was watching.

She noticed because she had learned to wait, to perch quietly in the places others hurried past, and watch for God's presence.

The others saw the bird as a coincidence.
Hadassah saw it as confirmation.

"Every time that bird shows up," she whispered once to the little girl beside her, "I believe Heaven's leaning close."

The child's eyes widened.

"But why doesn't it stay for the whole service?"
Hadassah smiled, gently and knowingly.

"Because sometimes, child... the Spirit just wants to see who came for Him, not for the show."

That bird became her barometer.

When it came, her spirit soared.

When it didn't show up in the first notes of praise... she prayed harder.

And then a Sunday dawned, no bird. Not a flutter, not a note, though the songs of worship rose.

Not during the opening chorus.

Not during the bridge.

Not even during the key change, when voices swelled and hands lifted.

Hadassah felt it immediately.

So did Elias, though he couldn't name what was missing.
The air didn't breathe the same.

That afternoon, as chairs folded and the sanctuary emptied,

Hadassah stayed behind. She watched the window like a widow waiting for her beloved.

"Lord," she whispered, "who didn't come for You today?"

She didn't know it yet...
But five rows ahead of where she had sat this morning, a man nursing a wound the church hadn't seen.

A wound dressed in pride.
A calling twisted by performance.
He used to worship first.
He used to clean, to play, to pray.
He used to see the bird, too.

But now?
Now he was building something else entirely.
And Heaven was about to interrupt him.

Watching

Luke 19:40 (KJV)
"And he answered and said unto them, I tell you that, if these should hold their peace, the stones would immediately cry out."

Reflection Reading:

Hadassah carried a gift many overlook, the gift of watching. In a world eager for noise and activity, she noticed the small details: the chipped tile, the hidden tears, the bird that only came when worship was pure. Her eyes weren't fixed on performance or routine, but on the presence of God.

The bird became more than a creature in the window; it became a signpost of Heaven's nearness. While others rushed past, Hadassah recognized that God often reveals Himself in quiet, subtle ways. Her faith was not in the bird itself, but in the God who chooses to confirm His presence in whispers and in wonders.

But when the bird didn't come, Hadassah wasn't shaken — she was driven deeper into prayer. Instead of questioning

God's faithfulness, she questioned her community's readiness. She understood a vital truth: the Spirit moves where hearts are yielded, not where performance takes the stage. Worship is not about filling a service, but about drawing Heaven's gaze.

For Hadassah, the absence of the bird was not despair — it was a call. A reminder that God still seeks true worshipers who come for Him, not for the show.

Prayer Focus:

Lord, open my eyes to see Your presence in the small and quiet ways. Guard my heart from treating worship as routine or performance. Teach me to come for You alone — not for the noise, not for the show, but for Your glory. And when Your presence feels distant, let my response be to seek You more, not less. Amen.

Journaling Prompts:

What small details in my daily life might the Holy Spirit be using to remind me of His nearness? _______________________________
____
____

Am I more concerned with outward performance or with truly hosting the presence of God? _______________________________
____
____

How do I respond when I don't feel God's presence — with discouragement, or with deeper prayer and seeking? ___________
____
____

What does it mean for me personally to "come for Him, not for the show"? ____
____
____
____

Beyond the Walls Action Step:

Practice faithfulness and obedience in a small, steady way this week. Pick one threshold — your home, workplace, or even a daily routine — and commit to pray over it consistently. Ask God to make it holy ground. Then, be obedient in one simple act: invite, encourage, or serve someone who crosses that threshold. Through your faithfulness, you create space for God's presence to meet them.

Part Two

The Rogue Servant

Jalen: The Performer Who Forgot to Worship

1 Samuel 15:22
""Tell me," Samuel said. "Does the LORD really want sacrifices and offerings?
No! He doesn't want your sacrifices. He wants you to obey him."

Ephesians 5:21
"Submit to one another out of reverence for Christ."

There was a time when Jalen served with joy.

He swept floors with quiet excellence.
Laid hands on the hurting.
Played the keyboard when no one else would.

He didn't need the spotlight,
He carried the Spirit.

But slowly... something shifted.
Applause became his appetite.
The spotlight, his fuel.
He stopped arriving early to pray.
Started leaving before clean-up.
If he wasn't asked to lead, he wasn't interested in showing up.

Worship turned into performance.
Service soured into ego.

The final crack came one Sunday morning.
He interrupted Pastor Elias mid-sermon to "correct
doctrine." And to be fair... he wasn't entirely wrong.

But the spirit behind the words?
Arrogant.
Unyielding.
Wounded beneath the bravado.

Later that week, Elias met with him privately.
Correction was offered, gently, truthfully, & in love.
But Jalen wasn't ready to receive it.
"I serve God, not man," he snapped.

Elias didn't react in anger. He simply nodded and replied,
"And yet... Jesus knelt and washed feet." Jalen left that day.

Not just the meeting.

The church.

Weeks passed. Then months. And the church? It didn't
collapse. In fact, it began to breathe again.

But something... someone... was missing. 

One Wednesday evening, during intercessory prayer, a visitor slipped into the back row.

Head bowed. Shoulders low.
Jalen.

He didn't ask for a microphone. Didn't touch the keyboard. Didn't speak.

He just came and wept.
Not for fanfare. Not with repentance on display.
Just surrender. After the service, Hadassah approached silently, laying a hand on his back.

"You're not forgotten," she whispered. "You're just being reshaped."

That next Sunday, Jalen returned.
Not to lead. Not to preach.

To clean the bathrooms. And for the first time in a long while, he smiled while doing it. Because this time, he wasn't serving to be seen.

He was worshiping again, through the water and the rag.

And Heaven... noticed. 

That same Sunday, a woman stepped into the sanctuary and didn't make a sound, but her presence rang louder than any hymn.

Recognition

1 Samuel 15:22

"Does the LORD really want sacrifices and offerings? No! He doesn't want your sacrifices. He wants you to obey him."

Ephesians 5:21

"Submit to one another out of reverence for Christ."

Reflection Reading:

Jalen's story is the story of many servants who begin with a pure heart but slowly trade Spirit-led worship for self-driven performance. He once swept floors, played instruments, and laid hands in prayer out of love for God— but the applause of people became louder than the whisper of the Spirit.

When correction came, he resisted. Pride cloaked his wound. His gifts, once surrendered, became tools for recognition. But God, in mercy, allowed him to be broken— not to destroy him, but to reshape him.

The turning point wasn't a grand moment of public repentance. It was a quiet surrender. Jalen returned not with a microphone in hand, but with a rag and a bucket. Worship was reborn in hidden service. The bathrooms became his altar, and a smile returned to his face because his heart had returned to the Lord.

This chapter reminds us that God does not delight in performance without obedience. True worship is not measured by the stage, the spotlight, or even outward sacrifice—it is measured by the heart that submits, serves, and obeys. Heaven notices humility long before it notices talent.

Prayer Focus:

Father, forgive me for the times I have sought the approval of man over the approval of heaven. Teach me to serve with humility, joy, and obedience. Reshape my heart where pride has crept in, and let my service—whether seen or unseen—rise to You as worship. May I find joy again in serving You, not to be noticed, but to be faithful. Amen.

Journaling Prompts:

Where in my life have I been tempted to seek recognition rather than quiet obedience? ______________________________
____
____

How do I respond when I am corrected—do I resist, or do I allow God to reshape me? ______________________________
____
____

What "bathroom-level" acts of service has God placed before me that I've overlooked because they seemed too small or hidden? ______________________________
____
____

How can I reframe my daily acts of service (even unseen ones) as worship to God? ______________________________
____
____

What steps can I take to guard my heart so that service stays Spirit-led, not self-driven? _______________

____

____

Beyond the Walls Action Step:

This week, choose one unseen act of service you can do quietly—without announcing it, without seeking credit, without recognition. Clean, give, help, or encourage in a way that points only to Jesus. As you do it, pray: "Lord, this is my worship to You." Let humility become your testimony, showing the world that obedience is greater than performance.

Part Three

Return to the Altar

Selah: The Musician Who Went Silent

Galatians 6:9
"Let us not be weary in doing well: for in due season we shall reap, if we faint not."

When the worshipers and the workers move as one 
Heaven doesn't just visit. It dwells.

Selah.

Years ago, her fingers had danced across that piano.
Her melodies had ushered hearts into sacred spaces.

Not through showmanship, but through a holy hush few
could replicate.

But something happened.
A wound.
Not loud or public, just deep.

A moment of correction that turned into a fracture.
And in time, her music stopped. She didn't walk away from
God. She just... left the room.

And now, she stood at the back, scanning the sanctuary  like a woman searching for permission to hope again.

Jonas saw her first.

He nudged Elias gently. "It's her."

Elias nodded but didn't rush. He waited for the Spirit's timing, not his own.

His sermon was ready. Notes prepared. Scriptures marked. But as he stepped up, something shifted.

He laid the notes aside.

He opened instead to 2 Chronicles 7:14 and read slowly:

"If my people, who are called by my name, will humble themselves and pray…"

His voice trembled, not from fear, but from weight.

"…and seek my face and turn from their wicked ways…"

Selah's head dropped.

"…then I will hear from heaven, and will forgive their sin, and will heal their land."

Elias stepped down from the platform.

"Today, there is no sermon. Only an invitation."

No music. No prompting.
And yet... the people moved.

Jonas came first, not in brokenness, but in unity. He knelt beside others.

Priscilla, the gentle doorkeeper, followed, laying her hands quietly on bowed shoulders.

Andre rose from his row, leading his children to the front.

Talia prayed for her family aloud, for the first time in months; her voice didn't tremble.

And then... Selah stepped forward.

Not to the altar. To the piano.
It sat just as she had left it, covered by the cloth from her last Sunday. Hands trembling, she lifted the cover.

She turned to Elias: "If there's room in the Body for a builder who bulldozed...
a single mom who doubted...
a father afraid to lead...
then maybe there's room for the sound again."

Elias nodded. "Play when you're ready."

She sat.
No spotlight. No prelude.
Just one quiet chord.

Then another.

Then...like rain on parched ground, the melody returned.

Soft.
Sacred.
Healed.

It wasn't music born from performance.
It was worship born from restoration.

The sound became a prayer.

The prayer became unity.

A unity, a revival.
Not the kind with lights and fog machines.

But the kind with tears.

Testimonies.

And trembling joy.

They didn't rush out after service.

They stayed.

Ate together. Held each other's children.
Shared their stories like warm bread passed from hand to
hand.

That night, Elias remained at the altar alone, whispering
thanks.

Behind him, Selah sang. Not lyrics, just sound. A refrain only
Heaven could fully understand.

And then he saw her.
A figure by the back doors.

Elderly. Silent.

Wrapped in the same familiar shawl from years ago. She
hadn't left the faith. The faith had just gotten... loud.
Too loud to hear her still, small prayers.
But now, she had returned. And with her came something
deeper still.

Because before the songs are played, before the altar is
rebuilt, before revival roots itself in the ground,
There is always one faithful intercessor.

And her name... was Priscilla.

Wounded

Galatians 6:9

"Let us not be weary in doing well: for in due season we shall reap, if we faint not."

Reflection Reading:

Selah's silence wasn't rebellion; it was a wound. The piano sat covered, not because she lost faith, but because her heart was fractured. Sometimes the deepest scars in the body of Christ are not from those who leave God entirely, but from those who step back quietly, carrying pain the church doesn't always see.

When she returned, it wasn't through a sermon or performance, but through surrender and unity. The altar was rebuilt not by one person's strength but by the body moving together—Jonas kneeling, Priscilla interceding, Andre leading his children, Talia praying aloud. When Selah uncovered the piano, her trembling hands signaled something greater than music: the healing of a heart, the restoration of worship, and the birth of revival rooted in unity.

Her story reminds us that true worship is not born out of
talent but restoration. It's not the stage lights or a polished
performance that invite Heaven's presence—it's the
humility of a people who seek His face together. And when
the weary return, when the broken are restored, when the
silent sing again, Heaven draws near.

Prayer Focus:

Lord, heal the silent places in me where pain has caused me to step back. Restore joy where it has grown weary. Teach me to see others with compassion and to make space for their return. May my worship rise not from performance but from restoration, and may unity in Your body bring revival. Amen.

Journaling Prompts:

Have I ever stepped back from serving or worshiping because of hurt or weariness? How did it affect me? _______________
____

What does Selah's return teach me about God's heart for restoration?_______________________________________
____
____

How can I be more sensitive to those in my community who have grown silent in their service or worship? _____________
____

In what ways is God calling me to return to the "altar" in my own life? ____
____
____

Where do I see the need for unity and shared surrender in my family, church, or community? ___________________________

____

____

Beyond the Walls Action Step:

Reach out to someone who has "gone silent"—a friend who stopped serving, a neighbor who stepped back from faith, or someone weary in life. Offer encouragement, a listening ear, or an invitation to join you in prayer or fellowship. Don't pressure them to perform; simply create space for restoration. Your love may be the nudge that helps them return to their altar.

Part Four

The Keeper of the Door

Priscilla: The Intercessor Who Kept the Threshold Holy

Matthew 25:23 (NLT)
"Well done, my good and faithful servant. You have been faithful in handling this small amount, so now I will give you many more responsibilities. Let's celebrate together!"

1 Corinthians 15:58 (ESV)
"Be steadfast, immovable, always abounding in the work of the Lord, knowing that in the Lord your labor is not in vain."

Hadassah had never truly left the Church.
She simply slipped quietly from its rhythms when the noise grew too loud and the spotlight too sharp.

For years, she prayed from her living room chair.
Bible worn. Knees worn. Faith unshaken.
Her tea sat beside her each morning on a napkin that read:

"He hears even this."

No one saw her in the building anymore.

But Heaven never stopped hearing her name in the courts of
intercession.

She prayed for Jonas before he repented.
She prayed for Elias before he called them back to the altar.
She prayed for Selah when her song was still silent.

Then one quiet morning, she heard a whisper in her spirit that
startled her:

"The Body is healing. Go be part of the breath again."

So she came.
Slowly.
Quietly.
Unannounced.

Wrapped in the same shawl she wore the last time she'd stood
in that sanctuary.

Priscilla saw her first.
Her eyes filled with tears.
"Savta Hadassah…"
Hadassah chuckled, steady and soft.
"Still holding the door for wandering sheep, I see."
Priscilla helped her find a seat near the back.
But Hadassah hadn't come to sit long.

She came to pray.

To pass on.

To ignite.

That evening, she returned for the Sunday Evening Prayer gathering.

No announcement.
No title.
Just presence.

When she prayed, the room didn't get louder.
It got still. Not because her voice thundered. But because her words carried weight, like dew on parched earth. She didn't ask for a ministry.

But one found her.

Young mothers gathered in her home.
Teen girls sat at her feet. Widows who had stopped attending returned just to sip tea and hear her speak of the God who still sees the secret place.

She didn't need a platform.
Her prayers were the platform.
And they had already changed the atmosphere.

Priscilla, moved by Hadassah's return, began asking others to help at the door, not just to greet, but to intercede.

She anointed the thresholds with oil each week, whispering,
"Let this doorway be holy ground."

She trained others, not in how to smile, but in how to see:
The broken.
The new.
The nearly-walking-away.

Before long, the entrance became a ministry of its own.

People said they felt peace the moment they stepped inside.
They weren't imagining it. It had been prayed for, week after
week.

Then, one Thursday afternoon, as golden light spilled across
Cedar Hill, a knock came at Hadassah's door. A girl stood
there, seventeen, eyes downcast, shoulders curled inward.
"I don't know how to pray out loud," she said. "But I think... I
want to know Jesus for real."

Hadassah smiled and gently reached for her hand.
"Then come sit with me. We'll pray in silence, until your yes
grows loud."

That Sunday, Alina entered the sanctuary. Still hesitant. But
heart wide open. She sat beside Hadassah.
She didn't sing, not yet. But she watched the worship like
someone seeing light for the first time.

She was no longer on the outside. But just as she settled in...
A knock came at the side door during Sunday night prayer.

Priscilla slipped away from the circle to answer.
She brushed her palms against her skirt.
Opened the door.
And gasped.

It was a woman she'd seen every week from across the street,
at the diner, always watching, never entering.
Eyes red.
Hands trembling.
"I don't know why I came," she whispered.
 "But... I think I need to stop watching. And start walking in."
Priscilla didn't hesitate.
She opened the door wide.
Not just into the building, but into something holy.

Faithful

Matthew 25:23 (NLT)
"Well done, my good and faithful servant. You have been faithful in handling this small amount, so now I will give you many more responsibilities. Let's celebrate together!"
1 Corinthians 15:58 (ESV)
"Be steadfast, immovable, always abounding in the work of the Lord, knowing that in the Lord your labor is not in vain."

Reflection Reading:

Priscilla's strength was not found in a microphone or a spotlight but in quiet, steady faithfulness and obedience. She showed up week after week, anointing thresholds, whispering prayers, and noticing souls who might have slipped away unnoticed. These weren't grand gestures — but they were holy, because they were obedient. Faithfulness is not about being seen; it's about being steadfast when no one else is watching. Obedience is not about convenience; it's about responding when God says "stay at the door," even if you long to move elsewhere. Priscilla's ministry reminds us that what seems small in man's eyes carries eternal weight in God's kingdom. The peace people felt when entering Cedar Hill wasn't decoration — it was the fruit of her obedience.

The door became a place of encounter because she was faithful in the hidden place. And Heaven still celebrates those who keep their post, no matter how ordinary it seems, because God's glory often enters through the doors guarded by unseen faithfulness.

Prayer Focus:

Lord, teach me the beauty of steady faithfulness and quiet obedience. Help me embrace the places You've assigned me, whether they seem small or hidden, and to serve with joy as if every moment matters to You — because it does. May my life be marked not by applause, but by faithfulness to Your call. Amen.

Journaling Prompts:

Where in my life is God asking me to practice simple, steady faithfulness? ____________________________ ____________________

____

Do I sometimes overlook the importance of small acts of obedience? Why?________________________________

____

How can I shift my focus from being noticed by others to being faithful before God? ___________________________

What "thresholds" in my life need to be prayed over and kept holy through obedience?________________________

____

Who might God be calling me to notice and welcome in, simply through my faithfulness at the door?________________

____

This week, choose one unseen act of service you can do quietly—without announcing it, without seeking credit, without recognition. Clean, give, help, or encourage in a way that points only to Jesus. As you do it, pray: "Lord, this is my worship to You." Let humility become your testimony, showing the world that obedience is greater than performance.

Part Five

The One Watching

Jessa: The Outsider Who Dared to Step In

Romans 15:7
"Wherefore receive ye one another, as Christ also received us to the glory of God."

Jessa had seen them for years.
From behind the foggy diner window, she watched Cedar Hill Community Church empty every Sunday afternoon.

She noticed everything.

Who hugged long. Who left fast.
Who left only tracts and tight smiles. At first, it was just curiosity. Then it became something else.

A hunger.
A whisper. 
A longing that refused to quiet.

She saw it all.
Jonas, storming out one week, returning the next with different kind of strength. Pastor Elias, praying in the parking lot with a grieving couple, hands locked like anchors.

Hadassah, the shawled woman, holding a teenager's hand like
she was guarding treasure.
Each Sunday, something in Jessa ached.
"If that's real...then why does it feel so far away?"

She came close a dozen times.
Stepped onto the sidewalk.
Paused at the edge of the lawn.
Heart pounding.
But always...turned back.
Until the night she couldn't.

She didn't know what pulled her across the street.
Only that something inside her cracked open, and the only
place that felt remotely safe was the sanctuary she had never
dared to enter.

Mara opened the door. No questions. No pressure.
Just a simple welcome. "You're right on time."
And for the first time in years, Jessa walked in.

The sanctuary was quiet. A few scattered worshippers
whispered prayers into the room like incense.

Jessa didn't kneel. Didn't cry. She just sat.

And in the silence, she whispered:
"God... if You're really here, don't let me leave the same."

No thunder. No shaking.
But when she opened her eyes, Selah was sitting beside her.

"Hi," Selah said gently.

"You've been near us for a while now, haven't you? Watching from across the street?"

Jessa nodded, embarrassed.
"I didn't want to pretend. I needed to know it was real, before I stepped in."

Selah smiled. "That's what makes it real. You didn't come for the show. You came for Him."

Then came the rest.

Elias passed by with warm tea.

Jonas cracked a joke.

Mara brought a bulletin.

Jessa didn't have words...only awe.
She looked around the room at these people she'd observed from afar. They weren't polished. They were pierced. Wounded. Redeemed. Real.

And then it hit her...
She belonged. Before she believed. Not in doctrine. Not yet. But in love. In invitation. In the quiet proximity of people who carried God like oil in worn clay jars.

She came back the next week.
And the next.

Eventually, she joined Mara at the door.
Not because she had answers.

But because she remembered what it felt like to wonder if
anyone would notice you crossing the threshold.

Weeks later, Elias asked her to share on Testimony Sunday.
Jessa stood, trembling, a napkin in hand.

Four words written on it:
"I was always watching you."
She looked out at the faces she once watched from behind
glass.
"I thought I needed to understand before I stepped in.

But what I needed...was to be welcomed."
Silence.

Then tears.
Then clapping. Then arms around her shoulders like blessings
made of flesh.
In the third pew, Hadassah smiled quietly and whispered:
"He heard even this."

What Jessa didn't know was that her single step of obedience
shook something loose in the room again.
Not just in the pews...
But in the hallway where a teenager named Alina was about to
discover her voice.

Afraid

Romans 15:7

"Wherefore receive ye one another, as Christ also received us to the glory of God."

Reflection Reading:

For years, Jessa stood at a distance, watching the Church like an outsider looking through fogged glass. She studied their flaws, their failures, and their faith. And in her watching, something grew, a hunger that no performance could satisfy. When she finally crossed the street, she didn't find a perfect people. She found a broken and redeemed family who welcomed her before she fully believed. What drew her in wasn't flawless sermons or polished programs; it was the authenticity of people who carried their scars with grace and offered her love without conditions.

Her story reminds us of the profound truth of the gospel: belonging precedes believing. People don't always need answers first — they need to know they're welcomed, seen, and loved. Christ calls His Church to radical hospitality, to receive others as He received us: in our mess, in our hesitation, in our searching. One small "yes" from an outsider can ignite revival within the whole body, because welcome is the doorway to worship.

Prayer Focus:

Lord, open my eyes to those who are watching from the edges. Give me the heart of Christ to welcome them with love before they have it all figured out. Teach me to carry Your presence with authenticity, so that my life reflects not perfection, but redemption. May every step of hospitality point them not to me, but to You. Amen.

Journaling Prompts:

Who in my life might be "watching from a distance," curious about faith but afraid to step closer? ___________________________

____

____

Do I sometimes expect people to believe or behave a certain way before I welcome them in?______________________________

____

____

What does it mean for me personally to extend belonging before belief?____

____

____

How can my own scars and authenticity help others see that God is real through me?_____________________________________

____

____

How has someone's welcome or invitation made a difference in my walk with Christ?_________________________________

____

Beyond the Walls Action Step:

This week, intentionally invite someone who may feel like an outsider — a neighbor, coworker, classmate, or even someone sitting quietly at church. Extend hospitality without strings: share a meal, offer a ride, invite them to sit with you, or simply listen to their story. Don't pressure them to believe first; simply let them belong. Your welcome may be the bridge God uses to bring them home.

Part Six

The Almost Amen

Alina: The Silent One Who Found Her Yes

1 Timothy 4:12
"Let no one despise your youth, but be an example to the believers in word, in conduct, in love, in spirit, in faith, in purity."

Alina had always felt like a question mark in a world full of exclamation points.
She never doubted that God was real.
She just doubted He wanted someone *like* her.

She had grown up in the background listening, observing, nodding when expected.
She knew the songs.
She could recite the verses.
But when it came time to step forward, to speak, to say Amen out loud, her heart would hesitate at the edge.
Frozen just before surrender.

She didn't know why.
Fear? Maybe.
Unworthiness? Definitely.
She was the girl who prayed in silence because she didn't trust her voice to hold steady.

Then Hadassah came.
And the silence started to feel less like shame and more like a
sanctuary. Each week, they sat together. Hadassah didn't
push. Didn't prompt. She just modeled stillness. Confident in
God, who doesn't require loudness to listen.

Then one evening, Hadassah pressed something into Alina's
hand.

Her old napkin.

"He hears even this."
Alina didn't cry loudly. Just... long.

And in that soft breaking, she whispered her first out-loud
prayer:

"God... I don't want to watch anymore. Teach me to walk."

That week, she joined the youth group. Not sitting in the back,
one foot out the door, but to stay. Pastor Elias, seeing the fire
flicker in her, asked her to lead the prayer at the next youth
night.

She panicked. "I can't. What if I mess it up?"
Jonas overheard and chuckled.

"I mess it up every week. That's why I let God do the heavy
lifting."

Selah sat with her during rehearsal.
"Don't pray to impress. Pray to invite."

The night came.
The fellowship hall filled with teens, some laughing, some skeptical, all waiting for more than just snacks and music. Elias gave her the nod. Alina walked slowly to the mic. Hands trembling. Voice thin.

She closed her eyes. And then...she paused. Not from hesitation, but reverence.

Then she spoke:
"God... You don't need my perfect words. Just my honest ones. So here I am. Not trying to be strong, just trying to be real. And I ask that You help us love each other enough to follow You together."

It wasn't loud. It wasn't polished. But it was pure.
And the Spirit filled the room like a gentle wind on dry land.

That night, two classmates came up to her.
"Can we pray again, sometime? Not because we need a leader, but because we found a friend who believes."

Alina didn't realize it yet. But she had just sparked something. Not a program. A movement. A movement of teens who weren't hungry for pizza and games. They were hungry for Jesus. And they wanted to find Him, together.

From the back of the room, Elias whispered to Jonas:
"She's going to change this town. Jonas smiled.
"She already changed the room."

As the youth night wrapped up, Alina got a text.
It was from her friend, the one she'd prayed for, in silence, for years.

She wasn't inside. Didn't trust church people. Didn't trust prayer. But she was outside.

Waiting. Watching. Wondering.

Alina turned to Hadassah, holding up the napkin with trembling fingers.

"Do you think He hears this, too?"
Hadassah smiled.

"He always does."

And Alina... walked outside.

Silenced

1 Timothy 4:12

"Let no one despise your youth, but be an example to the believers in word, in conduct, in love, in spirit, in faith, in purity."

Reflection Reading:

Alina felt like a question mark in a world full of exclamation points. She knew the words of faith but hesitated to believe her voice mattered to God. Her silence was not unbelief, but fear wrapped in unworthiness.

Through Hadassah's quiet companionship, Alina learned that stillness is not shame—it can be sanctuary. When she whispered her first prayer aloud, it wasn't eloquence that drew Heaven close, but honesty. God wasn't waiting for perfect words; He was waiting for her yes. When she finally spoke publicly, her prayer was simple, raw, and trembling. Yet it was precisely that authenticity that opened the door for others to encounter the Spirit. Two classmates sought her out, not because she was polished, but because she was real. What Alina didn't realize was that her hesitant "amen" became the spark of a movement—an example that boldness doesn't always sound loud. Sometimes it sounds like quiet honesty that invites others to follow Jesus together.

Her story reminds us: obedience is not measured by volume, but by surrender. Even a trembling "yes" can shift a room and set hearts on fire.

Prayer Focus:

Lord, thank You that You hear every whisper and honor every trembling "yes." Forgive me for the times I've believed my voice or my faith wasn't enough. Teach me to walk in bold obedience, not relying on perfect words, but on Your Spirit moving through honesty. Use even my small steps to spark faith in others. Amen.

Journaling Prompts:

Have I ever felt like my voice, gifts, or prayers didn't matter to God? How has that shaped my faith? ______________________________
____

What does it look like for me to offer God not perfect words, but honest ones?____
____

Where might the Spirit be inviting me to step out in obedience, even if my voice shakes? ___________________________________
____

Who in my life might be waiting, watching, for me to live out an authentic faith? ____
____

How can I encourage younger believers (or those hesitant in faith) to know their "yes" matters to God? ______________________

____

____

Beyond the Walls Action Step:

This week, choose one way to say a quiet but bold "yes" outside of church. Pray aloud for a friend, share a Scripture with a classmate or coworker, or invite someone to join you in prayer or worship. Don't wait until you feel polished—let your obedience, however small, open space for the Spirit to move.

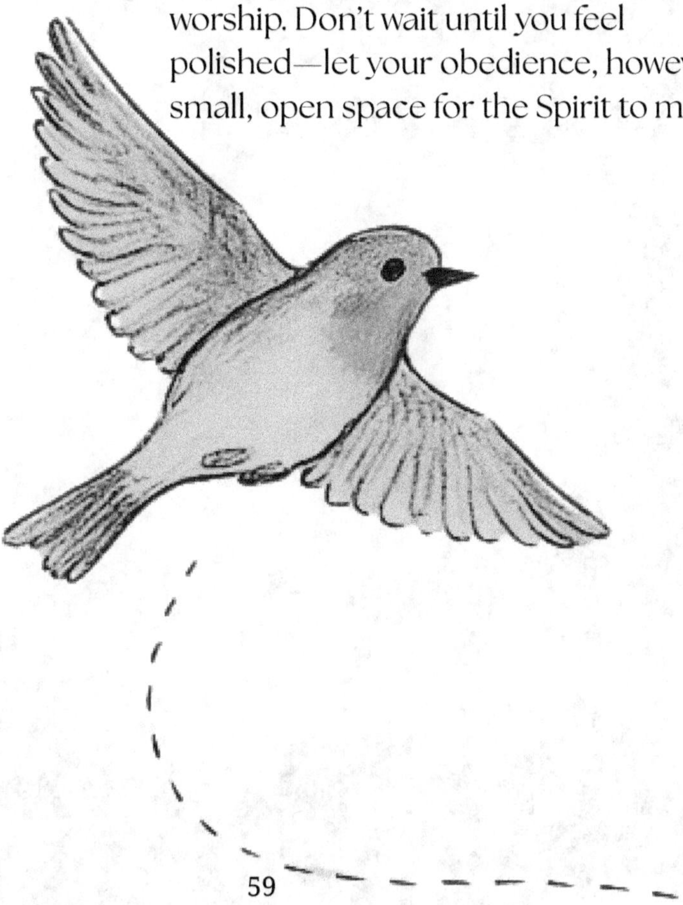

Part Seven

The Outside Invitation

Miah – The Skeptic Who Still Showed Up

Matthew 5:14–16
"You are the light of the world. A city that is set on a hill cannot be hidden… Let your light so shine before others…"

Alina brought a friend.

She didn't over-explain. Didn't promise perfection. Just a quiet offer: "Come if you want. It's not perfect. But it's honest."

Miah didn't do church. Not since her mother's breakdown.
Not since her father's slow, silent departures.
But something in Alina's voice felt different. Not like a pitch.
More like a promise.
So she came.

Miah didn't sing. Didn't close her eyes during prayer.
But she noticed. She noticed the old woman with the cane, lifting her hands like worship cost her something. She noticed the usher, shaking every hand like each one mattered. She noticed the worship leader, crying more than performing.

She noticed Elias, too. He didn't preach like a man trying to win. He preached like someone who had to eat the truth before serving it.

After the service, Miah sat on the front steps of the church, elbows on her knees.

"Why'd you bring me here?" she asked. Alina shrugged, simple and sincere. "Because I knew He was already waiting for you."
Miah didn't know what to say. But that night, she dusted off a Bible she hadn't touched in years. Just to see if it still opened.

It did. And inside... a card.
Her name. Her handwriting. From a different church, a  different life. She'd never seen it before.

But God had.

The next Sunday, Miah came again. Then someone else came, with a different friend. And then another. What Alina had started with one quiet "yes" was becoming something bigger. Not a crowd. A collection. Not of numbers...but of stories. And one of those stories? Was about to wreck them all. In the best, most holy way.

Skeptisism

Matthew 5:14–16
"You are the light of the world. A city that is set on a hill cannot be hidden… Let your light so shine before others, that they may see your good works, and glorify your Father in heaven."

Reflection Reading:

Miah didn't come because she trusted church — she came because she trusted Alina's honesty. Her skepticism wasn't about God's existence, but about His people's authenticity. And what moved her wasn't perfection or polish, but quiet faithfulness. She noticed the cost of worship in an old woman's lifted hands. She noticed sincerity in Elias's preaching. She noticed honesty in tears that outshone performance.

Her story reminds us that light doesn't argue with the dark, it simply shines. Miah wasn't convinced by explanations; she was compelled by examples. Alina's simple "come and see" opened the door, but it was the church's lived authenticity that made her stay.

The gospel invitation doesn't always begin with theology or debate. Often, it begins with an encounter, with people whose lives carry the fragrance of Christ. For skeptics like Miah, one honest friend and one open door can be the difference between staying away and daring to step in.

Prayer Focus:

Lord, help me to shine with authenticity, not performance. Give me courage to invite others, even skeptics, to simply "come and see." Teach me to trust that Your Spirit is already at work in their lives long before I speak. May my faith be honest enough to draw others closer to You. Amen.

Journaling Prompts:

Who in my life might be skeptical about faith, but still watching to see if it's real? _______________________________________
____

Do I sometimes over-explain when God may be asking me to simply invite? ____
____

What are the small, authentic ways I can let my light shine before others? ____
____

How has someone else's lived example of faith impacted me more than their words? ________________________________
____

What would it look like to extend an invitation not to perfection, but to honesty?______________________ ______________________

____

____

Beyond the Walls Action Step:

Think of one friend, coworker, or family member who may be skeptical of faith but open to honesty. Offer them a simple, pressure-free invitation — to church, to coffee, or to pray together. Don't promise perfection. Promise presence. Trust that God is already waiting for them, and that your role is simply to shine His light through faithfulness and authenticity.

Part Eight

The Gathering of Dust and Fire

Ben: The Veteran Who Thought He Had to Fix it First

Psalm 147:3
"He heals the brokenhearted and binds up their wounds."

Revelation 12:11
"And they overcame him by the blood of the Lamb, and by the word of their testimony..."

They came slowly...Then all at once.
First Miah. Then the boy in the hoodie, who never made eye contact. Then a woman with a baby on her hip and a bruise blooming on her cheek. Then a man with too many tattoos and not enough peace.

They didn't all come on Sunday. Some wandered in on Wednesday nights. Others found the church through food pantry pickups, whispered rumors, or 1 a.m. texts that read: "I don't know who else to call."

Selah, once hidden behind closed doors, now led worship with her whole heart.

Tommy, once too busy for small talk, now arrived early, stacking chairs with quiet joy.

Hadassah prayed over every pew before the lights even flickered on.

They weren't trying to grow a church. They were just becoming one.

And with every soul that entered, messy, raw, unfinished... something shifted. Like dust dancing in the morning light. Like fire rising from forgotten embers.

Ben, the quiet vet who had sat on the back row for months, finally asked to speak. He didn't make it halfway through his story before his voice broke. No one flinched. No one judged. They gathered around him, arms on shoulders, tears on shoulders, bearing witness without needing answers.

When he finally whispered "I thought I had to fix everything before I came..."

Elias answered without hesitation "You're not the fixer, brother. You're the found."

That night, the service didn't end with a song or a benediction. It ended with silence. Holy. Weighty. Still. As if Heaven itself had pulled up a chair.

They didn't know what to call what was happening. "Revival" felt too clean. Too rehearsed.

This wasn't loud.

Wasn't staged.

It was breath. It was brokenness. It was belonging.

And just when they began to settle, to feel safe again in the rhythm of restoration...

She walked in. The one name they hadn't spoken in months, maybe even years. The one memory they'd tucked into corners too sacred to disturb. And she wasn't alone.

"Unfixed"

Reflection Reading:

Ben's story reminds us of one of the greatest lies the enemy tells: "You have to fix yourself before you come to God." For months he sat quietly, believing that his wounds, his failures, and his past disqualified him. But the Church is not a gathering of the fixed, it is a gathering of the found.

When Ben finally spoke, it wasn't eloquence that broke the silence, it was honesty. His raw admission, "I thought I had to fix everything before I came," was not weakness, but worship. In that moment, the body of Christ became what it was meant to be: a family that bears one another's burdens, a place where testimony and tears carry as much weight as sermons and songs.

The Spirit moved not because they organized revival, but because they made space for brokenness. Dust danced in the light, and fire rose from forgotten embers. True revival is not rehearsed; it is raw. It comes when people stop pretending and start belonging. And in that belonging, healing flows.

Prayer Focus:

Jesus, thank You that I don't have to be fixed before I come to You. You are the Healer, the Restorer, the One who binds up my wounds. Teach me to rest in being found, not striving to fix myself. Help me to share my testimony with humility and courage, trusting that You use my scars as a witness of Your grace. Amen.

Journaling Prompts:

Have I ever believed the lie that I must "fix myself first" before coming to God or His people?________________________________

____

What burdens am I still carrying alone that I need to lay down at His feet?____

____

How does Revelation 12:11 remind me of the power of my own testimony?____

____

Who in my community might need to hear me say, "You don't have to be fixed first — you just have to be found"? ________________

____

____

What would it look like for me to help create space where broken people feel safe to belong before they are "finished"?

____

____

Beyond the Walls Action Step:

This week, share one piece of your testimony with someone not the polished version, but the real, honest part that shows where God has met you in brokenness. Remind them, through your story, that we overcome not by being perfect, but by the blood of the Lamb and the word of our testimony. In doing so, you open a doorway for others to realize they don't have to fix themselves first they just have to be found.

Part Nine

❧❧❧❧

The Name We Don't Say

Marla: The Prodigal Who Came Home

2 Corinthians 2:7–8
"Ye ought rather to forgive him, and comfort him...confirm your love toward him."

Ephesians 4:32
"Be ye kind one to another, tenderhearted, forgiving one another, even as God for Christ's sake hath forgiven you."

The doors creaked open during the second verse of the final worship song. Heads turned, subtly at first. Then not so subtly.

Selah's fingers faltered on the keys. Hadassah froze mid-prayer. Even Elias looked twice.

There she was. Marla James.

The woman whose scandal had nearly split the church. The one who once led. The one who lied. The one who disappeared.

And she was holding the hand of a teenage girl. Her daughter.
No one said her name anymore. It was safer that way, tidier.
But now she stood on sacred ground. Face uncovered. Eyes
searching.

Elias stepped down from the pulpit slowly. The sanctuary felt
like a rubber band stretched to its limit.

No script. No plan. Only one question hanging in the air:
What does the Church do with a prodigal when the pain is still
fresh? Marla didn't speak. She didn't walk forward. She didn't
beg. She just looked, toward Elias, toward Selah, toward the
faces she once called family.

And then, quietly, she slipped into the very last row. Bowed her
head. No altar call. No spotlight. No performance.
Just silence.
And then...a single tear.

Her daughter, the one no one knew she had, sat beside her,
eyes darting around the room, body stiff with panic, as if ready
to run.

And then...Miah stood. 

Yes, Miah: the diner watcher. The new believer. The one who
knew what it felt like to wonder if grace still had room.
She didn't say a word. She just walked to the back, and sat
beside them.

That was the sermon.

And now the whole church had to decide: Would they let the old wound rule? Or would they let the Light in?

Elias returned to the mic. Voice steady. Hands trembling. "Church... what we do next tells Heaven whether we've really been changed."

But not everyone stayed.
Near the aisle, Jonah stood. Arms folded. Jaw clenched.
He had served for years. Led studies. Organized outreach. Sat at hospital bedsides. But as he stared at Marla, weeping in the back pew, something in him hardened. He didn't move toward her. Didn't bow his head. Didn't whisper forgiveness. He shook his head. "You can all hug her if you want," he muttered, loud enough. "But don't expect me to pretend this is okay."

Tommy turned, voice low. "Brother, don't do this." Jonah's eyes flashed. "She destroyed this place once. I won't let her do it again." Elias opened his mouth to speak, but Jonah was already moving. Not toward Marla. Not toward the altar. Out the door.

It slammed.
And the sanctuary held its breath.

Hadassah's eyes brimmed. Selah's hands hovered over the keys. Marla's shoulders collapsed, as if the sound of the door had closed on her, too.

Elias swallowed hard. He knew there would be a cost to grace. He hadn't expected to pay it so soon. And he felt the floor shift beneath him.

Not the wood. Not the nails. The foundation. The one he thought they'd rebuilt. And he wondered, could a house this divided ever truly stand?

He turned toward the pulpit again, heart pounding. Their yes to grace had cost them Jonah. And as he sank into the front pew, he saw an envelope tucked beside the Bible he'd left earlier. City seal. He didn't open it. Not yet. But a chill passed through him. As if grace wasn't the only thing about to be tested.

Unforgiven

2 Corinthians 2:7–8
"Ye ought rather to forgive him, and comfort him...confirm your love toward him."
Ephesians 4:32

"Be ye kind one to another, tenderhearted, forgiving one another, even as God for Christ's sake hath forgiven you."

Reflection Reading:

When Marla walked back into the sanctuary, she carried more than her daughter's hand — she carried the weight of her past. The pain she left behind still pulsed in the room. Old wounds resurfaced. Memories whispered. The church faced the question every community eventually does: Will we make room for the prodigal, even when grace costs us something?

Some hearts bent low, ready to embrace her. Others hardened, unwilling to forget what had been broken. Forgiveness is rarely neat. It is costly, messy, and often resisted. Yet Jesus Himself makes no secret of His heart: we are to forgive as we have been forgiven.

Marla didn't beg or perform repentance; she simply showed up. Sometimes the bravest act of faith is walking into the

place where you are least certain you'll be welcomed. And sometimes the truest act of obedience for the church is to embrace the one who returns, even when it stings.
The cross is proof: grace always costs something. The only question is whether we are willing to pay that cost so redemption can take root.

Prayer Focus:

Father, thank You for forgiving me when I least deserved it. Give me the courage to extend the same mercy to others, even when it costs. Heal my wounds so I don't let bitterness rule me. Teach me to confirm love to those who return, and let my forgiveness become a witness of Your grace. Amen.

Journaling Prompts:

Who in my life have I struggled to forgive because their wound still feels fresh?______________________________________

____

What holds me back from extending grace: fear, pride, or the pain of the past?____________________________________

____

How does remembering my own "prodigal moments" help me extend forgiveness to others?______________________________

____

____

Where might God be inviting me to "confirm love" to someone
who has returned in humility?______________________________

____

What cost am I willing to pay for grace to be real in my
community? ____

____

____

Beyond the Walls Action Step:

Reach out to someone who has been
absent, estranged, or avoided because
of past mistakes. Offer a word of
kindness, a meal, or simply presence —
not to excuse sin, but to extend grace.
Let your life declare that forgiveness is
possible, and that the door home is
never fully shut when Christ is the one
holding it open.

Part Ten

The Door Opener

Tommy: The Loyal One Who Chose Grace

John 10:9 – "I am the door: by me if any man enter in, he shall be saved, and shall go in and out, and find pasture."

Matthew 23:13 – "But woe to you, scribes and Pharisees, hypocrites! For you shut the door of the kingdom of heaven in people's faces. You yourselves do not enter, nor will you let those enter who are trying to."

Tommy had always been the dependable one.

He stacked chairs after potlucks. Filled the baptistry before services. Checked the furnace in winter, the swamp cooler in summer. He liked tasks with clear edges. Jobs he could finish with his hands. Ways he could prove he mattered. But when it came to people, he struggled. Not when they cried. Not when they failed. Not when they crossed the line.

He was the first to say "You know better."
The first to vote for removal "for the sake of order."

So when Marla walked in that Sunday, it rattled something

deep in him. He saw Jonah, jaw locked, arms folded. He heard him mutter: "Don't expect me to pretend this is okay."
And Tommy felt it too, the sting of memory. The meetings. The lies. The leadership fallout. He remembered how proud he'd felt slamming the door on the gossip...And how sick he'd felt wThen he saw Marla's daughter, eyes wide, body tense, waiting to see if anyone would move. That's what did it.
Then came Elias's voice, cracking over the mic:

"Church... what we do next tells Heaven whether we've really been changed." And before his heart caught up, Tommy's legs were already moving. He walked to the back, laid his hand on the doors, and pushed them wide open. Wide Open. But he didn't step through.

He stood there for a long time after Jonah left. Long after the room had quieted. Watching the parking lot swallow his brother. Eyes burning. Because he knew, there would be more Jonahs. People who couldn't forgive. People who wouldn't stay. People who'd call him soft. Naive. Wrong. But he also knew this: He was done closing doors.

Later that week, Elias found him in the foyer, tools spread out, tightening the hinges. Tommy didn't look up. "They got loose," he muttered.

Elias nodded. "They do that when you actually use them." They both chuckled. Then Elias's voice dropped, low, reverent.

"Thanks for being the first one to open them."

Tommy swallowed hard. Nodded once. Then kept working.

That Sunday, he sat in the back. Not to hide, but to watch.
He saw Selah, eyes closed, singing like she meant every word.
He saw Hadassah, praying over Marla's daughter. He saw
Alina, arms wrapped around Miah. He thought of the fights
they'd still have. The wounds still healing. The people who
might never come back. But he also saw the Spirit, Moving.
Free. Uncontained. And he realized: The doors weren't just
open for Marla. They were open for everyone.

Including him.

As he gathered his tools to leave, something caught his eye
on Elias's chair. An envelope. Official seal. City of Cedar Hill.
He turned it over slowly, a weight settling in his gut.
He exhaled. They'd opened the door for Marla. But there
were harder doors ahead.

Because tomorrow...it wouldn't just be about keeping the
doors open. It would be about what to do when there were no
walls left at all.

Bold

John 10:9

"I am the door: by me if any man enter in, he shall be saved, and shall go in and out, and find pasture."

Matthew 23:13

"But woe to you, scribes and Pharisees, hypocrites! For you shut the door of the kingdom of heaven in people's faces. You yourselves do not enter, nor will you let those enter who are trying to."

Reflection Reading:

Tommy was steady, dependable, the man you could count on to set up the chairs and check the furnace. But when it came to people, he leaned toward rules over grace. He'd been proud of shutting the door once, until he realized he'd closed it on people who needed it most.

When Marla returned, scarred by scandal but carrying her daughter, Tommy felt the old instinct to guard the threshold. But then he saw her daughter's wide, waiting eyes. In that moment, obedience to grace mattered more than his comfort with order. So he did what Jonah could not: he opened the door.

Tommy's story reminds us that the Church's power is not in how well it controls the doors, but in how faithfully it keeps them open. Yes, grace is costly. Yes, some will leave. But keeping the door open is the way of Christ — because He is the Door. To slam it shut is to miss the heart of the gospel.

Grace always stretches us. But it also saves us, not just the prodigal who walks back in, but the loyal servant who finally learns that obedience is greater than sacrifice, and love is greater than rules.

Prayer Focus:

Lord, thank You for being the Door that was never closed to me. Forgive me for the times I've shut others out instead of opening wide with grace. Give me the courage to hold the doors open, even when it's costly, and to trust that You are strong enough to guard Your house. Teach me to choose grace over fear, and obedience over comfort. Amen.

Journaling Prompts:

Have I ever closed the door on someone because of their past or my own fear of being hurt again?

Do I lean more toward order and rules, or toward grace and restoration? Why?

What does it mean for me to "keep the door open" in my family, friendships, or church?________________________________

____

How has God's grace kept the door open for me, even when I didn't deserve it? ________________________________

____

What door is God asking me to open right now, even though it feels costly or risky? ________________________________

____

Beyond the Walls Action Step:

Look for someone who may feel shut out — someone who hasn't been welcomed, trusted, or invited in. Reach out with a text, a meal, or an invitation. Keep the door open through grace, not because it's easy, but because Christ kept it open for you.

Part Eleven

The Church Without Walls

The Church That Would Not Be Contained

1 Corinthians 3:11
"For other foundation can no man lay than that is laid, which is Jesus Christ."

Acts 5:42
"And daily in the temple, and in every house, they ceased not to teach and preach Jesus Christ."

The town hall was packed.

Elias stood at the podium, a stack of carefully prepared papers in his hand, flanked by Tommy on one side, Hadassah on the other. The city wanted to rezone the church property. "Civic improvement," they called it. A library. A walking path. More parking.

Progress, they said. But to those who worshipped in its walls, this wasn't just land. This wasn't just wood and nails. This was holy ground: Creaky. Worn. Sacred.

Elias had written a strong case. Planned every line. But as he looked out over the crowd, he folded the speech.
And spoke from the heart.

"We are not here to defend bricks. We are here to defend belonging. This church has always been more than walls. It's the place where the broken come back. Where prodigals find porch lights still burning. Where names once spoken in shame are spoken again in grace.

So do what you must with the land...
But know this: Cedar Hill's church doesn't live in drywall. It lives in us."

Some clapped. Some rolled their eyes.
The city voted. The building fell.

But the Body? The Body had already decided: if the building fell, the Church would rise.

The next few weeks were a whirlwind. Prayer meetings turned into planning sessions. Worship spilled into the park. The Table, where communion and meals met, moved to the town square.

But not everyone came along. Jonah never returned.
His absence was like a missing note in a hymn you know by heart. They felt it. Grieved it. Prayed for him, every time. And they kept going.

Marcus offered to clear the land. Ben volunteered his construction skills. Mara gathered the children under a

Elias had written a strong case. Planned every line. But as he looked out over the crowd, he folded the speech.
And spoke from the heart.

"We are not here to defend bricks. We are here to defend belonging. This church has always been more than walls. It's the place where the broken come back. Where prodigals find porch lights still burning. Where names once spoken in shame are spoken again in grace.

So do what you must with the land...
But know this: Cedar Hill's church doesn't live in drywall. It lives in us."

Some clapped. Some rolled their eyes.
The city voted. The building fell.

But the Body? The Body had already decided: if the building fell, the Church would rise.

The next few weeks were a whirlwind. Prayer meetings turned into planning sessions. Worship spilled into the park. The Table, where communion and meals met, moved to the town square.

But not everyone came along. Jonah never returned.
His absence was like a missing note in a hymn you know by heart. They felt it. Grieved it. Prayed for him, every time. And they kept going.

Marcus offered to clear the land. Ben volunteered his construction skills. Mara gathered the children under a

canopy and called it "Kingdom Tent." Selah's team wrote a
new song. Alina and Miah started a podcast.
Tommy built a pulpit from a tree stump. Marla and her
daughter found their place among them, learning, serving,
and healing with the rest.

It was raw. It was beautiful. It was alive. 

One night, under open skies and in folding chairs, Elias stood
and preached, eyes wet, voice strong. "This may not be the
sanctuary we remember...But maybe, just maybe, it's the
sanctuary God always intended."

And the Spirit moved. 

People brought blankets and questions. Testimonies.
Leftovers. Repentance happened in the middle of sidewalks.
Grace spilled over into alleyways. The gospel had left the
building, and found a field.

But even as the Body settled into this rhythm of revival, Elias
felt it. A weight. A whisper. A call. He looked out at his people,
God's people, faithful. Forgiven. Fragile. And deep in his
spirit, he knew: This field wasn't the final destination.
Something was coming. Or someone. Someone with news
that would change everything.

 Someone who wouldn't ask them to stay...

But to go.

Exposed

1 Corinthians 3:11

"For other foundation can no man lay than that is laid, which is Jesus Christ."

Acts 5:42

"And daily in the temple, and in every house, they ceased not to teach and preach Jesus Christ."

Reflection Reading:

When Cedar Hill lost its building, the people discovered what it truly meant to be the Church. Bricks and drywall had never been the foundation — Jesus Christ had. They realized the sanctuary wasn't a structure; it was a Spirit-filled people.

Elias's words echoed through the town: "We are not here to defend bricks. We are here to defend belonging." And with that, revival spilled beyond the walls. Worship filled the park. Communion was shared in the town square. Prayers rose in homes and alleyways. The gospel could not be contained, because the Spirit cannot be contained.

This moment reminds us of the early Church in Acts. When persecution scattered them, they carried the gospel into homes, streets, and cities. Revival has never been dependent on buildings, it has always been dependent on obedience.

The Church without walls is risky, raw, and uncomfortable. But it is also alive. It is here that testimonies shine brightest, that forgiveness is embodied, and that the gospel goes where it could not before. Sometimes God allows walls to fall so His people will finally step into fields.

Prayer Focus:

Lord, remind me that You are the true foundation of the Church. Thank You that Your Spirit cannot be contained by walls. Teach me to be faithful in the field, to carry Your presence into places that feel risky or unfamiliar. Let my life be a sanctuary where others encounter Jesus, whether in a building or on a street corner. Amen.

Journaling Prompts:

Have I ever confused the building with the Body? What does this chapter teach me about the true foundation of the Church?

____

____

____

Where might God be asking me to carry His presence outside the familiar walls of worship?_______________________________

____

____

How do I personally respond when the structures I rely on are shaken or removed?________________________

____

____

What would it look like for me to live as part of a "Church without walls" in my neighborhood, workplace, or community?

____

____

____

____

What risks might God be asking me to take so that the gospel reaches beyond comfort zones? _________________

____

____

Beyond the Walls Action Step:

Do one act of "church outside the walls" this week. Share a meal with a neighbor. Pray with someone in a public place. Start a Bible study at work or in your home. Take communion with your family around the dinner table. Show that the Church is not bound to a building, it is alive in you.

Part Twelve

The Stranger's Story

The Stranger: The Messenger Who Wouldn't Stay

Matthew 28:19–20
"Go ye therefore, and teach all nations... teaching them to observe all things
whatsoever I have commanded you..."

He didn't look like a preacher. Or a prophet. Or anything in between.

Worn jeans. A faded olive jacket, collar frayed. Boots caked with the dust of other towns, other fires. And eyes that held the quiet ache of a man who had seen too much, and written it all down.

He stood at the edge of the park gathering, journal pressed to his chest, head bowed slightly as worship rose into the dusk like incense. When the final Amen floated across the grass, Elias noticed him.

"You passing through?" Elias asked, voice warm but cautious. The man smiled. "Or maybe I was sent. Depends on who you ask." He held out the journal.

"I think you're supposed to read this."

Inside were stories. Names. Towns. Little churches, just like
Cedar Hill. Churches that lost their buildings...but found fire.
One in Idaho, meeting in a barn. One in Louisiana, gathering
by boat. One in Georgia, worshiping in an abandoned skating
rink. And at the very end of the journal, in simple script:
"When the building falls, the Bride still stands."
Elias turned the page and found a map:

Five towns. Circled in red.

"God's been waking people up," the stranger said. "But
they're scattered. He's looking for a church that's willing to
go, not just stay."

Elias closed the book slowly.
"Are you saying...?" The stranger nodded.

"I'm saying the harvest is outside your field."

That night, they met under the stars.
Selah. Hadassah. Tommy. Alina. Ben. Kendra. Marcus.
No stage. Just blankets and questions and wonder.
"I thought revival was here," Alina said.

Hadassah nodded gently.

"It is. But sometimes the spark has to be carried."
Elias looked down at the journal. Then back at the people
he'd walked with through fire and forgiveness. "What if God's
calling us to become the invitation?"

Silence.

Then Kendra whispered: "What if He's calling us to go before they ask for Him?"

And from that question, something new was born. Not a tour. Not a crusade. A caravan of obedience.

The stranger would go with them for a while. Then move on. That was always his way. A planter, not a builder. But Cedar Hill...would become both.

The next Sunday, they commissioned the first team.
They called it: **The Light Beyond the Hill.**
Just before they departed, the stranger handed Elias one final page.

Scrawled in bold ink:

"Make disciples, not just converts.
 Make families, not just churches.
 Make movement, not monuments."

And at the bottom:
Matthew 28:19–20.

They didn't know it yet. But what had begun in broken walls... would one day touch nations.

All because one small church said yes to becoming,
The Living Church.

Carried

Matthew 28:19–20

"Go ye therefore, and teach all nations... teaching them to observe all things whatsoever I have commanded you: and, lo, I am with you alway, even unto the end of the world."

Reflection Reading:

The Stranger didn't come to stay, he came to send. He carried a message Cedar Hill needed to hear: the harvest was bigger than their field. Revival wasn't meant to be hoarded; it was meant to be carried.

The journal he handed Elias told the same story in town after town, churches stripped of walls but ignited with fire. And in those stories was a simple truth: "When the building falls, the Bride still stands." What had been born in Cedar Hill through forgiveness, obedience, and costly grace was never meant to stop there.

This chapter reminds us that the Great Commission isn't optional — it is the heartbeat of the Church. The Spirit revives us so He can send us. He heals us so we can become carriers of healing. He sets us free so we can proclaim freedom to others. Cedar Hill had learned to be a church without walls. Now God was calling them to be a church without borders.

The Stranger's words echo across generations: "Make disciples, not just converts. Make families, not just churches. Make movement, not monuments." The Living Church doesn't stay, it goes.

Prayer Focus:

Lord Jesus, thank You that You never called me to stay comfortable, but to go obediently. Forgive me for the times I've settled for safe when You were calling me to send, serve, or speak. Make me a disciple who makes disciples. Let my life carry Your light beyond the walls, beyond the hills, into every place You send me. Amen.

Journaling Prompts:

Where have I been tempted to "stay," when God may be calling me to "go"?

What does it mean for me personally to live out the Great Commission in my daily life?

How can my scars and testimony serve as part of God's invitation to others?

Am I building monuments (comfortable structures) or movements (Spirit-led obedience)?______________

____

____

Who in my life is God calling me to disciple, not just invite?

____

____

____

Beyond the Walls Action Step:

Take one intentional step in the Great Commission this week. Share your testimony with someone outside the church, mentor a younger believer, or serve in a way that builds relationship rather than just numbers. Ask God to make you part of a movement, not just a moment — carrying His light into places that need to know He is real.

Epilogue

We Are the Church That Walks
An Anthem of the Living Church

Micah 6:8
"Mankind, he has told each of you what is good and what it is the LORD requires of you: to act justly, to love faithfulness, and to walk humbly with your God."

We are the Church that walks, not waits,
Not polished pews or golden gates.
But hearts made whole through sacred scars,
Lit lanterns held beneath the stars.

We are the hands, the feet, the call,
The whispered prayer in City Hall.
The soup, the song, the kneeling low, The healing tide in
hidden flow.

We are not steeples made of stone,
But voices raised when one's alone.
Not bound by doors or bells or books,
But grace that finds in unseen nooks.

We walk where aching souls reside,
Where truth's been buried, faith denied.

We knock, we wait, we dine, we stay,
We wash the feet the world throws away.

We build not temples proud and grand,
But tables wide with outstretched hands.
We plant, we water, trust the yield,
The harvest found in barren field.

We are the Church that walks, not hides.
The ones who stand when hope divides.
A Body living, led by flame,
With Christ alone our boast, our name.

So send us, Lord, we make this vow:
To be Your Church, not someday... now.

And when at last we gather near,
United hearts that cast out fear.
Let even Heaven lean in low,
And let Your Spirit's presence show.

As once before that window burned,
And now, at last, the bird's returned,
A holy sign to those who see:

"My Spirit dwells in unity."

Movement

Micah 6:8

"Mankind, he has told each of you what is good and what it is the LORD requires of you: to act justly, to love faithfulness, and to walk humbly with your God."

Reflection Reading:

The story of Cedar Hill ends not with walls rebuilt, but with a people remade. Their anthem is not about buildings, titles, or perfection, but about walking humbly with God wherever He leads.

To be the Church that walks is to remember that faith is not static, it moves. It serves. It listens. It opens doors. It plants seeds and trusts the harvest to God. This Church doesn't wait for the world to come in; it goes out with grace, justice, mercy, and love.

The anthem reminds us that revival is not a one-time event, it is a way of life. The bird returning to the window is not just a symbol of worship restored, but of unity lived out. The Spirit dwells in a people who walk in obedience, who love faithfully, and who carry Christ's presence into unseen nooks and forgotten places.

The Church that walks is not someday, it is now. And it includes us.

Prayer Focus:

Lord, make me part of Your Living Church. Teach me to act justly, love faithfully, and walk humbly with You. Let my scars become lanterns that light the way for others. May my life echo the anthem: not someday, but now. And may Your Spirit dwell in us in such unity that the world cannot help but see You. Amen.

Journaling Prompts:

What does it mean for me personally to "walk humbly with God" in my daily rhythms?_______________________________________

____

Where might God be calling me to act justly, love faithfully, or open doors for others?_______________________________________

____

How do I carry the anthem of the Living Church into my family, workplace, or community?_______________________________________

____

What step of obedience can I take today to move from being in church to being the Church that walks?_______________________

____

How might unity in the Body become a visible testimony of the Spirit in my town or circle?_______________________________

____

____

Beyond the Walls Action Step:

Take one step that embodies being the Church that walks. Serve someone practically. Speak encouragement where hope has been thin. Open your home for prayer. Share your testimony in a place you normally wouldn't. Live the anthem beyond the page, so that others see Christ not only in your words but in your walk.

The Living Church Chronicles

A Series of Redemption, Awakening, and the God Who Rebuilds What Breaks

The Living Church Chronicles follows the wounded, the wandering, and the quietly faithful as God breathes life back into His people, one soul at a time. In these interconnected stories, readers journey through shattered places, hidden scars, whispered prayers, and unexpected awakenings, witnessing how Christ restores not only individuals, but an entire church community.

Each book unveils a different angle of redemption and purposed assignments: the healing of broken hearts, the rekindling of forgotten callings, the courage to step into the unknown, and the holy work of rebuilding what the enemy tried to destroy. Through musicians and intercessors, pastors and prodigals, outsiders and servants, this series invites readers to behold the Church not as a building, but as a living, breathing people made whole by the grace of God.

From quiet restorations to outward mission, from the sanctuary to the hills beyond it, The Living Church Chronicles is a portrait of revival;

one scar, one story, one redeemed life at a time.

Book Two — The Light Beyond the Hill

The redeemed do not stay where grace found them.

In this next chapter of the journey, those who once hid in the shadows now step into their calling. With wounds still tender and faith newly awakened, they carry the flame of revival beyond the sanctuary walls, into the hills, the homes, and the hearts waiting on the other side of obedience.

A story of courage, calling, and the God who sends His people out.

Book Three — The House That Stands Again

Not everyone is sent out, some are called to stay.

Elias and the remnant rise from the ruins, rebuilding the sanctuary stone by stone, prayer by prayer. As old wounds surface and new strength is forged, they discover that restoration is holy work... and that a church rebuilt from ashes becomes a beacon for the broken.

A story of foundations, faithful hands, and the God who makes His house whole

About The Author:

Melissa Dyess is a woman who has known broken places and witnessed the beauty of God's rebuilding hand. A storyteller, mentor, and creator, she weaves her personal journey with her calling to help others heal and find purpose. Through Missing Piece Virtual Solutions and the dedicated team she serves alongside, Melissa helps authors, ministries, and visionaries bring their stories and assignments to life.

As a wife, mother, and Savta, Melissa carries a deep love for the generations God has placed in her life. Her passion for healing and restoration flows from her desire to see families walk in freedom, wholeness, and God's redeeming grace.

Her writing is shaped by the belief that scars tell the truth about God's faithfulness. Battle Scars of the Redeemed is Melissa's offering to the wounded and the weary: a reminder that redemption is not just possible, it is God's specialty. With every page, she calls His people back to hope, to worship, and to the God who sees, heals, and makes all things new.

MP Press is the publishing imprint of Missing Piece Virtual Solutions, a creative company committed to helping authors bring meaningful stories into the world. We focus on strategy, branding, and book marketing, working side-by-side with writers to strengthen their message, grow their reach, and connect their books with the readers who need them.

At MP Press, we believe publishing works best when it's done in community.

That's why we collaborate with a trusted network of professionals; such as Janelle Villiers Partnerships for coaching and author development, and Say That Publishing for editing, formatting, and production. Together, we offer a seamless, supportive experience that guides authors from idea to finished book.

MP Press exists to elevate powerful stories, empower writers, and help message-driven authors step confidently into their calling through the written word.

If you'd like to learn more about partnering with MP Press or exploring our collaborative services for authors and small businesses, we'd love to connect.

visit: www.mpvirtualsolutions.com